MARVEL AVENGERS

The THREAT of THANOS

By Arie Kaplan
Illustrated by Shane Clester

 A GOLDEN BOOK • NEW YORK

MARVEL © 2018 MARVEL marvelkids.com

rhcbooks.com

Educators and librarians, for a variety of teaching tools, visit us at RHTeachersLibrarians.com

ISBN 978-1-5247-6856-0 (trade) — ISBN 978-1-5247-6857-7 (ebook)

Printed in the United States of America

10 9 8 7 6 5 4 3

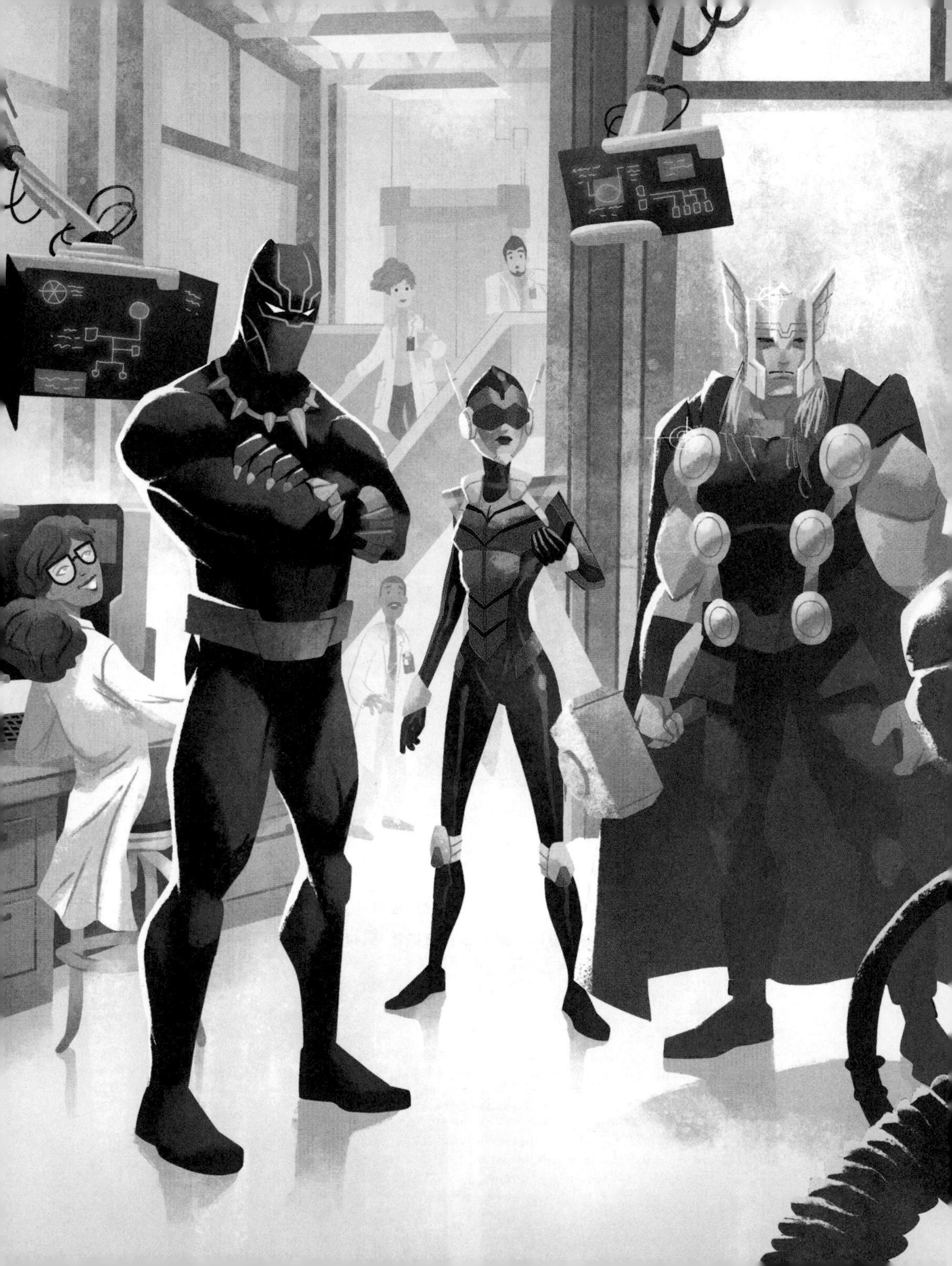

Earth's mightiest heroes, the **Avengers**, had been called to a laboratory in New York City, where scientists were studying a purple gem from outer space.

"It's giving off strange **energy waves**—almost like it's sending a message," Iron Man said.

"But who's it calling?" Wasp asked.

Suddenly, a portal opened and a fearsome figure appeared! He wore a **GOLDEN GAUNTLET** on one hand.

Black Panther growled.

THANOS!

"That gem is the final **Infinity Stone**," Thanos declared. "It is calling out to the other stones. With all six of them, I can **RULE THE UNIVERSE**!"

The heroes leaped into action,
ready to stop him.

"Avengers, **mind** your own business,"
the villain growled.

An invisible force pushed the heroes back!
"How did he *do* that?" Black Panther asked.

"Thanos is using the **Mind Stone**," Iron Man
explained. "It lets him push people around with just
his **thoughts**."

With the Avengers out of the way,
Thanos grabbed the **purple gem**.
He put it into his gauntlet, and the
golden glove started to **glow**.

"NOW *NOTHING* CAN STOP ME!" he roared.

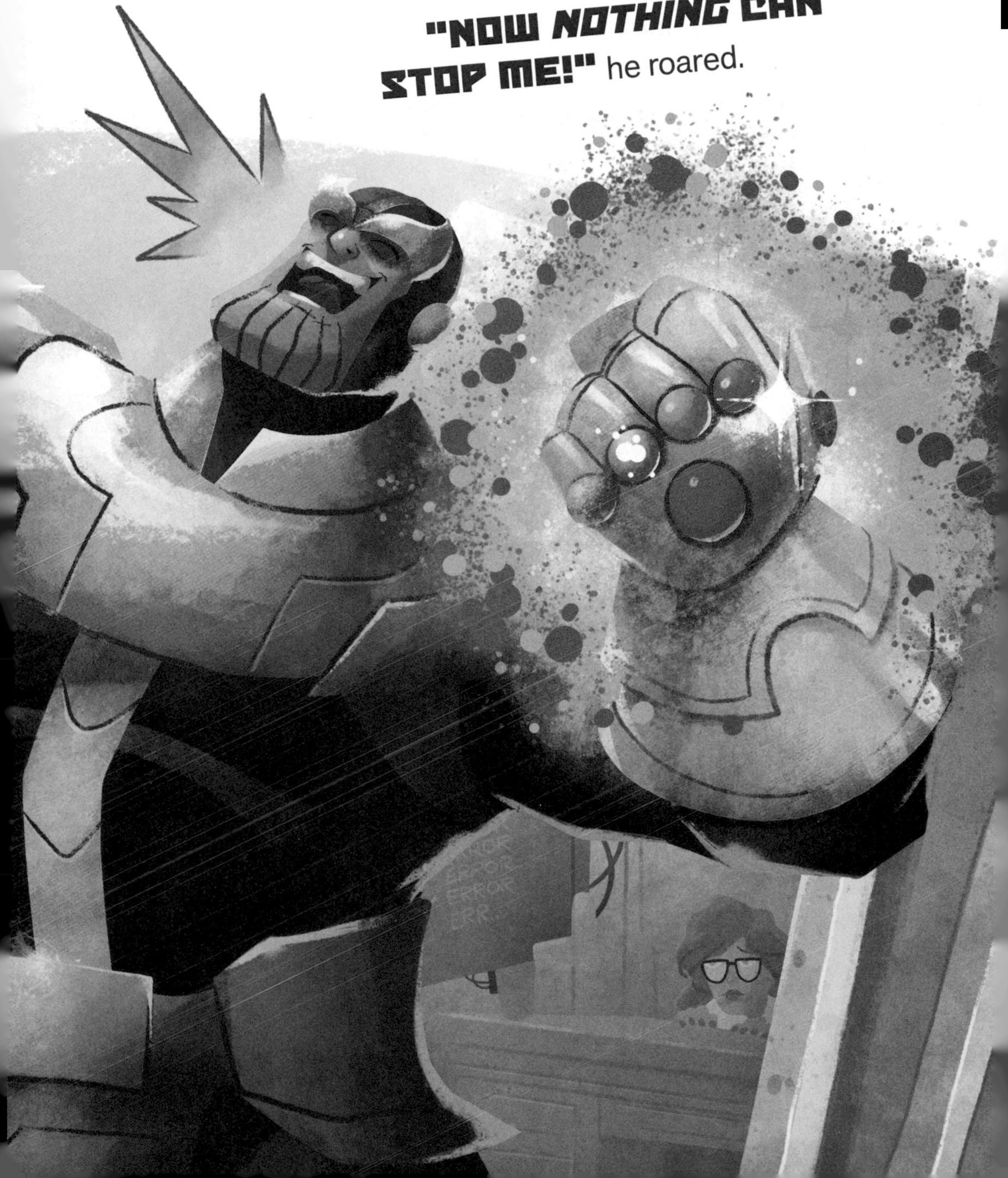

Soon the Avengers were back on their feet. As they approached Thanos, the building's **steel girders** started **moving**!

They wrapped around the **heroes**!

"Talk about a **tight squeeze**," said Black Panther.

Thanos was controlling the girders with the **Reality Stone**, which could make *anything* happen!

Iron Man used his powerful suit of armor to burst free.

Thor smashed the girders with his hammer.

Black Panther *sliced* through the steel with his *claws*.

And Wasp was too small and too fast to get caught.

Then the heroes tackled Thanos. But they couldn't remove his gauntlet!

Thanos zapped the heroes with bolts of alien energy.

ZZZT!

ZZZT!

ZZZT!

Earth's Mightiest Heroes fell to the ground.

"That was like getting hit with the world's biggest flyswatter!" Wasp joked.

"I'm feeling greedy," Thanos said to Thor. "I came here for the **gem**. But I think I'll *also* take your **hammer**!"

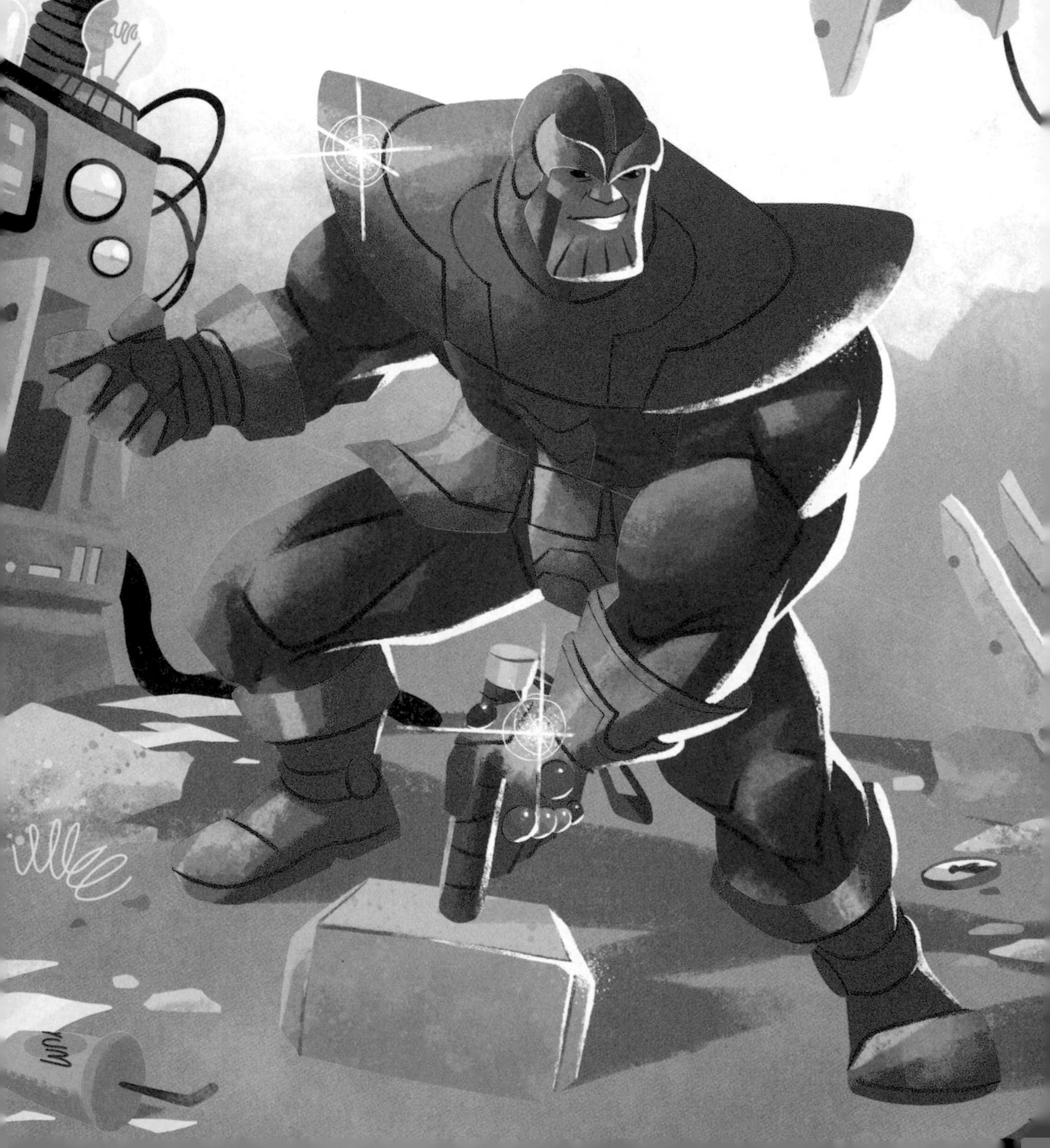

"You are not **worthy** to lift my mighty hammer," Thor said weakly. "Still, I dare you to **try**!"

Thanos grabbed the hammer, and Thor smiled. The blond hero reached out his hand, and the magic hammer returned to him.

It flew so quickly, it pulled the Infinity Gauntlet
right off the villain's hand!

Thanos was confused. "I don't understand,"
he said. "I zapped you with the **Power Stone**!"

"Yes, you did." Thor laughed.
"But I am the mighty Thor, and that
blast of energy merely **tickled**!"

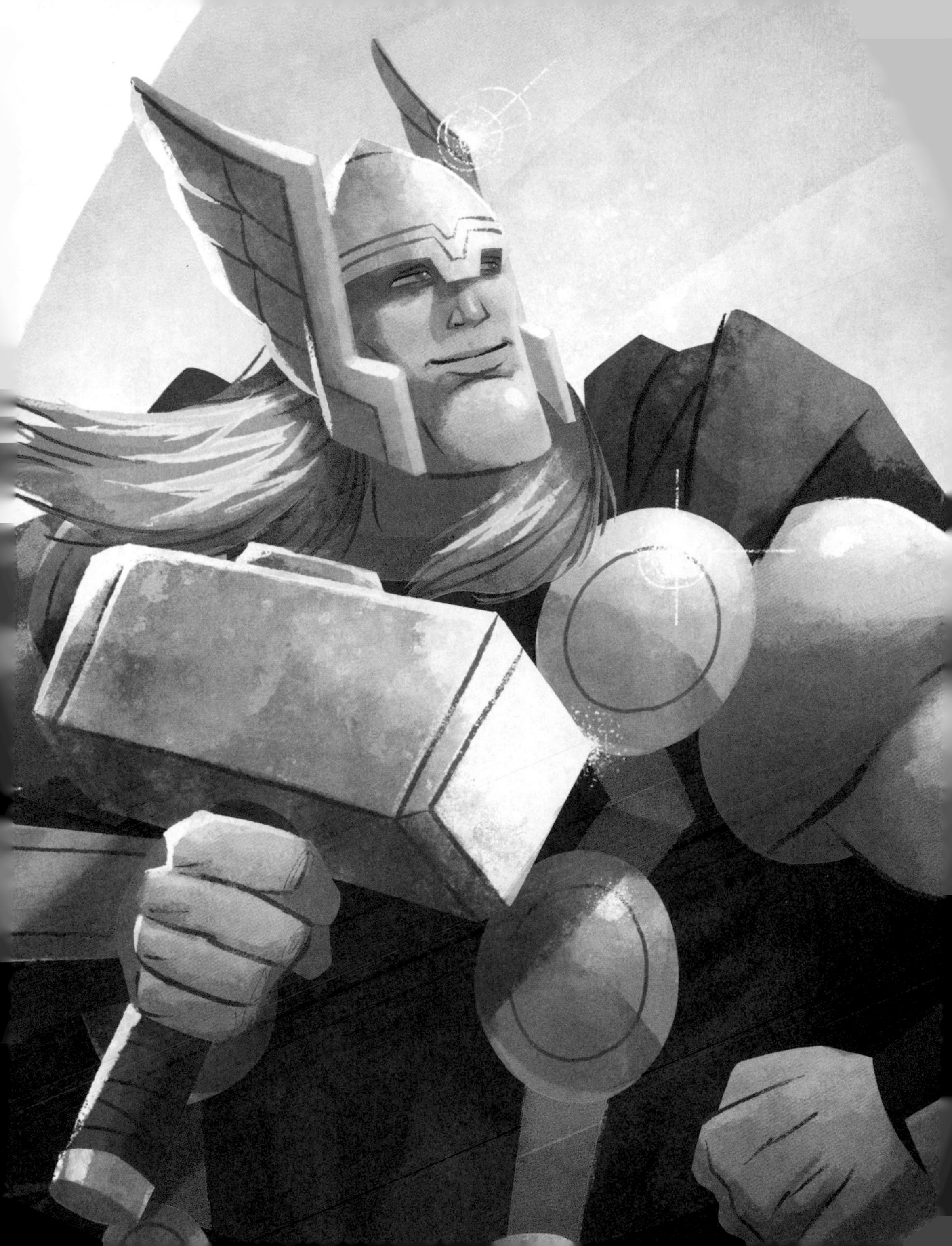

With Thanos under the Avengers' control, Iron Man contacted an interplanetary police force called the **NOVA CORPS**.

Nova Corps officers soon arrived to take Thanos
away to an alien prison.

"We will put the Infinity Gauntlet in a safe place,"
the officers promised.

With the day saved, the Avengers headed home. "Thanos was trying to complete his collection of Infinity Stones," Black Panther said to his friends. "But he was no match for *this* collection of heroes!"